Lola Dutch

KENNETH
AND SARAH JANE WRIGHT

BLOOMSBURY
NEW YORK   LONDON   OXFORD   NEW DELHI   SYDNEY

This is Lola. Lola Dutch.

Lola Dutch is a little bit much.

"Good morning, Bear!" said Lola.
"Today is going to be AMAZING!
I'm just BURSTING with ideas!"
"Goodness," said Bear. "First, might
we start the day with tea and toast?"

"Oh, no, I have grander ideas for breakfast," said Lola.
"Come, Bear, the kitchen awaits!"

Bear took a deep breath. Lola's ideas could be a bit much.

Gator wanted grits.
"What's grits without gravy?" asked Lola.

Pig wanted pastries.
"And hot cocoa with marshmallows, of course!"

Crane wanted crepes.
"One can never have too much whipped cream."

Bear braced himself.

"Lola Dutch, you are a little bit much," said Bear.

On their morning walk, Lola had another grand idea.
"Bear, I feel like a little light reading."

At the library, Gator studied the great inventors.

Pig observed the great chemists.

Crane researched the great writers.

Lola discovered the
great artists, and her
imagination ran . . .

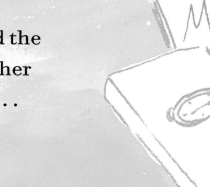

...wild.

As did her library card.

"Lola Dutch, this is just so much!" said Bear.

"Oh, Bear," said Lola, "I'm still BURSTING
with ideas! When we get home, it's time to PAINT!"

Gator gathered the brushes.

Pig mixed the paint.

Crane prepped the canvas.

"As the great artist said, 'Creativity takes courage!'
Forward, friends!"

et voilà !

Bear smiled. "Lola Dutch, you are just too much."

"Thank you, Bear. Next, I need to . . ."
"Oh, no, that's enough!" said Bear. "It's bedtime."

"All right," said Lola. "But first I need a bubble bath,

my favorite pajamas,

and a bedtime story."

Bear was very much
ready for bedtime.

Still, Lola felt one more
burst of creativity.

"Tonight I think we should sleep in something a bit more majestic," said Lola.

But Gator had cold feet. Pig snorted and snored.
Crane kicked in her sleep.

"This is ALL TOO MUCH!"

said Lola Dutch.

"What do you need?"
asked Bear. "More blankets? Fluffier
pillows? Fancier pajamas? Cookies and milk?"

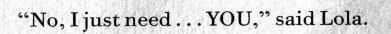

"No, I just need . . . YOU," said Lola.

"Lola Dutch, I love you so much."
"I love you so much, too, Bear."

Bear turned out the light.

"Good night," said Bear. "Something tells me
tomorrow is going to be another AMAZING day."

To our four "little-muches"
—Mom & Dad

First published in the United States of America in January 2018 by Bloomsbury Children's Books
www.bloomsbury.com

Bloomsbury is a registered trademark of Bloomsbury Publishing Plc

For information about permission to reproduce selections from this book, write to
Permissions, Bloomsbury Children's Books, 1385 Broadway, New York, New York 10018
Bloomsbury books may be purchased for business or promotional use. For information on
bulk purchases please contact Macmillan Corporate and Premium Sales Department at
specialmarkets@macmillan.com

Names: Wright, Kenneth, author. | Wright, Sarah Jane, illustrator.
Title: Lola Dutch / by Kenneth Wright ; illustrated by Sarah Jane Wright.
Description: New York : Bloomsbury, [2018]
Summary: It's the beginning of a new day, and Lola Dutch is bursting with creative ideas!
Even if her enthusiasm is a "bit much" for some, with the help of her animal friends she is inspired
to make every day amazing!
Identifiers: LCCN 2017019949 (print) • LCCN 2017037891 (e-book)
ISBN 978-1-68119-551-3 (hardcover) • ISBN 978-1-68119-552-0 (e-book) • ISBN 978-1-68119-553-7 (e-PDF)
Subjects: | CYAC: Creative ability–Fiction. | Enthusiasm–Fiction. |
Friendship–Fiction. | Animals–Fiction.
Classification: LCC PZ7.1.W79 Lo 2018 (print) | LCC PZ7.1.W79 (e-book) | DDC [E]–dc23
LC record available at https://lccn.loc.gov/2017019949

Art created with pencil, gouache, and watercolor • Typeset in Bodoni Six ITC Std
Book design by Donna Mark and Jeanette Levy
Printed in China by Leo Paper Products, Heshan, Guangdong
1 3 5 7 9 10 8 6 4 2

All papers used by Bloomsbury Publishing, Inc., are natural, recyclable products
made from wood grown in well-managed forests. The manufacturing processes
conform to the environmental regulations of the country of origin.

Research the artists and paintings who inspired Lola Dutch: Henri Matisse (1869–1954),
the Cut-Outs, 1940s • Claude Monet (1840–1926), *Bridge over a Pond of Water Lilies*, 1899 •
Pablo Picasso (1881–1973), *The Old Guitarist*, 1903–1904 • Gustav Klimt (1862–1918),
Portrait of Adele Bloch-Bauer I, 1907 • Vincent van Gogh (1853–1890), *The Starry Night*, 1889 •
Johannes Vermeer (1632–1675), *Girl with a Pearl Earring*, c. 1665 • Michelangelo (1475–1564),
The Creation of Adam, 1508–1512.